All Kinds of Babies

by MILLICENT E. SELSAM

Pictures by SYMEON SHIMIN

SCHOLASTIC BOOK SERVICES

NEW YORK · TORONTO · LONDON · AUCKLAND · SYDNEY · TOKYO

ISBN: 0-590-02348-9

Text copyright ©1967,1953 by Millicent E. Selsam. Illustrations copyright © 1967 by Symeon
Shimin. All rights reserved. Published by Scholastic Book Services, a division of Scholastic
Magazines, Inc.

20 19 18 17 16 15 14 13 12   9/7 0/8

Printed in the U.S.A.

07

All Kinds of Babies

This very minute, and every minute in every day, all kinds of babies are being born — crab babies, fish babies, insect babies, elephant babies, human babies, and many, many other kinds of animal babies.

Some kinds of babies start life looking like their parents.
You can guess that this fluffy ball of fur is going to be...

a grown-up cat.

You can't make a mistake
about a baby snake.

It grows and grows. The little snake grows into . . .

a big snake.

As this baby grows,
his neck grows longer
and his body gets bigger.
He will be...

a full-grown giraffe.

This baby has two little bumps that will grow
into two big humps. When it grows up it will be . . .

a grumpy camel.

When this baby is born, it has fur, teeth, and spines.
You know it is...

a porcupine.

This baby will one day
swing from tree to tree
like his mother
and father chimpanzee.

There are lots of babies that look like their parents, but...
there are some babies that don't look like their parents
at all — not even a little bit.

Here is one kind with a wiggly tail and no legs.

It lives in water and swims all day. As it grows,
it changes. Its tail slowly disappears.

Four legs grow.

Now it can hop about on land, or swim,
or sit on a lily pad and croak, like any full-grown frog.

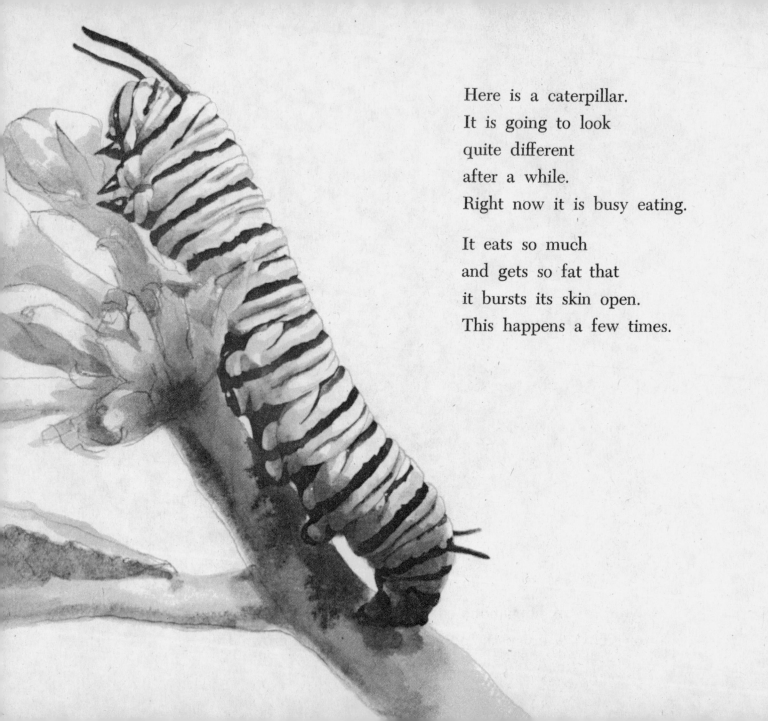

Here is a caterpillar.
It is going to look
quite different
after a while.
Right now it is busy eating.

It eats so much
and gets so fat that
it bursts its skin open.
This happens a few times.

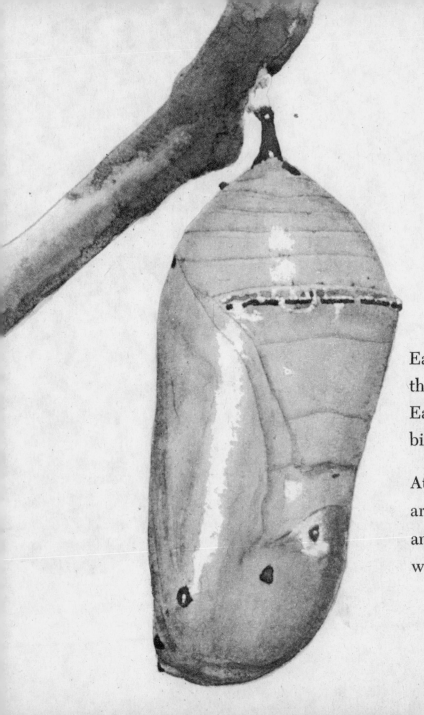

Each time, it wriggles out of
the old split skin.
Each time, it has a new and
bigger skin underneath.

At last it makes a hard covering
around itself
and takes a long rest
while it slowly changes into . . .

a beautiful, winged butterfly.

Baby eels look so different from their parents
that for a long time nobody knew whose babies they were.
They are as thin as leaves, and you can see right through
their bodies.
After a year they become narrow, long, and round.

They slowly change into these
full-grown, dark, slippery eels.

When crab eggs hatch in the water, they are the size
of tiny crumbs. If you look at them through a microscope,
you can see that they do not look at all like their
crab parents. They keep growing new shells and crawling out
of the old ones. Each time they look a little different.

After a month they look like crabs, but are still very tiny.
They are only this big 〓.

The little crabs will get bigger and bigger, and keep on making new shells and crawling out of the old ones many, many times. After a year they are full-grown crabs.

These little birds take a while to look like their parents.
See them swimming in the water.
Can you guess what they'll be?

Graceful white swans.

This baby once had pink skin and very little hair.
He weighed only one pound and was no bigger
than a newborn puppy. He is bigger now.
And someday he will weigh a hefty 400 pounds.
What will he be?

A great big bear.

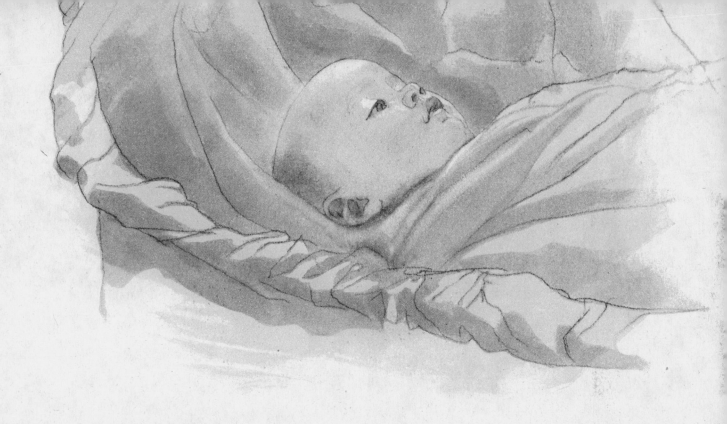

Here is another baby.
This baby will not become a bear or a crab or a butterfly.
This baby will grow up to be
a boy or girl like you.

The world is full of babies growing up.

Some start life looking like their parents.

Some babies don't look like their parents at all.
But no matter how they look when they are babies,
they will grow up to be the same kind of animals
as their parents.

A baby sea gull will not change into a penguin.
It becomes a grown-up sea gull.

A monkey's baby will always grow up to be a monkey —
never a horse.

Every kind of living thing in the world makes more
of its own kind. This is true of fish, insects, birds,
and every kind of animal.

This is true of everything that grows
in the world.